Fizzy Feet

Some other books by Margaret Ryan . . .

Hover Boy:
2: Beat the Bully
3: Missing Moggy Mystery

For younger readers . . .

The Canterbury Tales
1: The Big Sister's Tale
2: The Little Brother's Tale
3: The Little Sister's Tale

For older readers . . .

Operation Boyfriend

published by Hodder Children's Books

FIZZY FEET

MARGARET RYAN
iLLUSTRATED BY NiCOLA SLATER

Hodder
Children's
Books

a division of Hodder Headline Limited

For Donald, with love –
Margaret Ryan

Text copyright © 2002 Margaret Ryan
Illustrations copyright © 2002 Nicola Slater

First published in Great Britain in 2002
by Hodder Children's Books

The rights of Margaret Ryan and Nicola Slater to be identified
as the author and illustrator of this work respectively have
been asserted by them in accordance with the Copyright, Designs
and Patents Act 1988.

10 9 8 7 6 5 4 3 2 1

A Catalogue record for this book is available from the British Library

ISBN 0 340 80604 4

Printed and bound in Great Britain by
Bookmarque Ltd, Croydon, Surrey

Hodder Children's Books
A division of Hodder Headline Limited
338 Euston Road, London NW1 3BH

CHAPTER ONE

"DON'T HOVER!"

Has your mum ever said that to you, when you're lurking about in the kitchen, trying to sneak an extra chocolate biscuit?

Oscar Smith's mother said that to him too.

"Don't hover, Oscar."

His dad said it to him as well.

"Don't hover, Oscar."

His twin sisters, Evie and Angie, never stopped saying it.

"Don't hover, Banana Bonce!"

Because Oscar hovered a lot.

Not just in the kitchen, but in the

sitting-room, the bedroom, the hall, even in the loo. Oscar could hover anywhere. This was very embarrassing for his family because Oscar didn't hover like the rest of us. Oscar hovered three feet up in the air. Even higher if he put his mind to it.

Oscar's hovering worried his mum.

"I'm sure it can't be good for him," she said to his dad. "Perhaps we should take him to the doctor."

"No, no, he looks healthy enough," said his dad. "He'll probably grow out of it. I grew out of collecting stamps."

"I don't think that's quite the same," said his mum.

"'Course it is," said his dad. "Don't make a fuss. It's a phase he's going through. All boys go through phases."

Oscar's hovering worried his twin sisters, Evie and Angie.

"You're a weirdo, Oscar," they told

him. "Don't come anywhere near us when our friends are in. We don't want them thinking we're related to a nutter."

Oscar's hovering worried him too. He knew aircraft hovered. He knew spacecraft hovered. He knew hovercraft hovered. But he knew boys didn't. Usually. It just wasn't normal.

He had read books about what was normal for boys growing up. He knew all about squeaky voices. He knew all about hairy armpits. And – AAARGH – he knew all about boys suddenly liking girls. But nowhere, in any of the books, did it say anything about hovering up in the air. Nowhere did it say anything about a faint feeling of fizziness in the feet which got stronger and stronger till wheeeeee! LIFT OFF and there you were, three feet up in the air, arms flailing, toes dangling, saying hullo to the dust on top of the wardrobe.

Oscar knew it wasn't normal. That's why he did his best to hide it.

At home, it didn't matter too much. His family could see he wasn't ill, and soon got used to him hovering around. They picked up the ornaments and tables he knocked over, and tried to remember to open doors carefully, in case he was hovering behind them.

His mum gave him a duster to clean the cobwebs from the high corners, and his dad got him to hang pictures, but Evie and Angie got cross when he hovered in front of the television and they couldn't see their favourite programme.

It was tricky, too, when visitors came. Then, Oscar mostly kept out of sight. He would poke his head round the sitting-room door, say a quick hullo, and vanish before anyone noticed his head was much higher up than normal.

"He's such a quiet boy," explained his mum to Great Auntie Vera.

"Very shy," said his dad to Great Uncle George.

"Weirdo," mouthed Evie and Angie to each other behind everyone's back.

At school it was different. There, whenever Oscar felt the faint feeling of fizziness start in his feet, he clamped his legs round his desk and held on tight. This made his desk wobble, his face red, and his eyes bulge.

"Are you all right, Oscar?" Miss Cheevers, his teacher, asked when this happened.

"Fine," replied Oscar, through clenched teeth, and held on till the faint feeling of fizziness faded and the danger was past.

But it was becoming more and more difficult. The faint feeling of fizziness was growing stronger, and was happening oftener, and Oscar had to put lots of pebbles in his pockets to try to weigh himself down. Trouble was, now he could hardly move, and, when he did, he rattled.

"Screwball," said his classmates.

It was all very tricky.

The only place Oscar felt happy in school was the gym. There, whenever he felt the faint fizziness start, he could leap up a wall bar or a climbing rope and just pretend to be an idiot. The class laughed, but he got into trouble with the teacher if he was supposed to be playing rounders or basketball at the time. But it was worth it. What was the odd punishment exercise compared to being thought even more weird than he was.

And it would have gone on like that if it hadn't been for that fateful Tuesday.

Tuesday was Gym day, Oscar's

favourite day of the week. The day he could take off his jacket and trousers with the heavy pebbly pockets, and parade his knobbly knees in his school shorts. FREEDOM! It had been a great Gym lesson, too. Oscar leapt over the vaulting horse and did forward rolls like an Olympic athlete. He only had to leap for the wall bars once, and that was when Miss Cheevers wasn't looking.

Miss Cheevers was really pleased with his efforts.

"You worked hard in the gym today, Oscar," she said. "Well done. You can stay behind and put all the equipment away in the gym cupboard."

Oscar grinned. Everyone liked this job. If you took your time, and put the equipment away really slowly, you could miss at least fifteen minutes of Maths.

So Oscar stayed behind.

He put the equipment away very neatly then looked around him. The big gym was strangely quiet after the noisy class had gone. Oscar loved the silence, the space, the emptiness – so when the faint feeling of fizziness started in his feet, he did nothing. No leaping for a rope, no whizzing up the wall bars. He just let himself gently rise three feet into the air. Then he began to move, light and free, hovering faster

and faster up and down the gym.
It was wonderful. It was exciting.
It was exhilarating. Till . . .

"Oscar, what are you doing?"

Oscar turned to see Miss Cheevers
at the gym hall door. She was looking at
him strangely. Like she'd seen a ghost,
or a werewolf, or a vampire with
"I Like Teachers" written in blood on
his T-shirt. Her mouth fell open, her
eyes glazed over, and she sank to the
floor like a saggy old beanbag.

"Oh no," cried Oscar, hovering
to her rescue. "I think she saw me.
I think she's fainted. I think I've been
found out!"

CHAPTER TWO

When she'd recovered, Miss Cheevers reported Oscar to Mr Robertson, the head teacher. He calmed Miss Cheevers down and sent for Oscar's parents. Oscar was waiting for them in the head teacher's room when they arrived. They looked anxious, and slid into the room like they'd just been caught breaking a window. Oscar had a sudden vision of how they might have looked when they were at school. Pigtails and freckles for his mum and lots more hair to cover the bald spot for his dad.

"Do sit down, Mr and Mrs Smith," said Mr Robertson.

Oscar's mum and dad sat on the edge of their chairs beside Miss Cheevers. Only Oscar was left standing. He examined the picture of the school football team on the wall above Mr Robertson's head. He'd seen it millions of times, but it was suddenly very interesting.

Mr Robertson cleared his throat, looking over his glasses, and put on his head teacher's patient expression.

"Mr and Mrs Smith," he said. "Miss Cheevers has told me a very strange story. She says she found Oscar hovering in the gym today. Not ordinary hovering, you understand, but up in the air hovering. Defying gravity hovering. Now I know this sounds preposterous" – he ignored Miss Cheevers' glare – "but Miss Cheevers insists that it is true. What's more, so does Oscar. Can you comment on this? Has Oscar been learning Indian

15

rope tricks, without the rope? Is he an illusionist? Should he be on the television? There must be a logical explanation. Perhaps there's a funny bug going round that makes people see things?"

Miss Cheevers glared at him again. Oscar's mum and dad looked at each other, then at Oscar. Oscar shrugged. What could he do? Despite his best efforts, he'd been found out.

"It's true," his parents said to Mr Robertson. "Oscar can hover in the air. It just came upon him sudden like, a few weeks ago. Gave us the fright of our lives the first time. One minute he was standing on the carpet. Next minute he was hovering halfway up the curtains."

"See," said Miss Cheevers triumphantly. "A funny bug indeed!"

"But he's a quiet boy," said Oscar's mum. "And we didn't want to make a fuss. We didn't want people pointing at him in the street."

"It might just be a phase he's going through," said his dad. "He'll probably grow out of it." And he looked hopefully at Oscar.

Oscar shook his head, for the faint feeling of fizziness had started, and before their very eyes, he began to rise slowly into the air.

"See," cried Miss Cheevers again. "I told you so."

"So you did. So you did," muttered Mr Robertson, loosening his collar, and staring, trance-like, at Oscar. "How very unusual. How very unusual indeed. And tell me," he said to Oscar's mum and dad, "are his sisters similarly afflicted . . . I mean . . . affected."

"Oh no," said Oscar's parents. "They're perfectly normal."

Oscar sighed. How could anyone

think that Evie and Angie, with their pink hair, their green eye-shadow and the tiger transfers on their bums, were perfectly normal!

Mr Robertson came out of his trance, adjusted his glasses, and was suddenly brisk.

"What we have here," he said,
"is a very unusual boy. Very unusual
indeed. Too unusual to stay at this
school. This is a school for normal,
I mean *ordinary*, I mean, children
who don't have special gifts. Oscar
obviously has a special gift."

"You wouldn't think it was so special
if your sisters called you a weirdo, and
you had to go round weighted down
with pebbles," muttered Oscar.

Mr Robertson ignored him. "Gifted
children," he went on, "should go to a
school where their gifts are recognized.
Now I'm going to tell you something
very few people know." And he lowered
his voice and looked about furtively.

"There is such a school not far from
here. People think the school is just for
extra-bright children, but it's more than
that. It's for children with special gifts.

Unexplained gifts. For some mysterious reason, we have a lot of these children around here, and Oscar is obviously one of them.

"The school is called the School Of Greatly Gifted Youth, or S.O.G.G.Y. for short. I shall telephone the head teacher, Madame Estella Carella, right away and tell her to expect Oscar tomorrow."

Finally he turned to Oscar.

"What do you think about that, Oscar? No more secrecy. You'll be with people who understand your gift and can help you develop it. I'm sure it will be a weight off your mind."

"And my body," grinned Oscar. "Now I can get rid of all these rattly pebbles. Now I can hover whenever I like. Now I can be normal."

CHAPTER THREE

Evie and Angie were extremely huffy when they heard that Oscar was going to the School Of Greatly Gifted Youth.

"Why aren't *we* greatly gifted, then?" they asked their mum and dad. "We're his sisters. His *older* sisters. It's not fair. Didn't you feed us plenty of fish when we were little? Fish is supposed to be good for brains. Or carrots. Didn't you feed us carrots? They're supposed to make you see in the dark."

"But you never liked fish," said their mum. "You both said you could feel them still wiggling in your stomachs."

"And you always picked the carrots

out of the stew," said their dad. "And pinged them at each other."

"Well, you should have insisted we ate them," stormed the twins. "That's what parents are supposed to do. We could have been geniuses by now."

"Or big brainy rabbits that can see in the dark," grinned Oscar.

The twins threw their cream buns at him. Oscar ducked and the buns splattered against the kitchen wall.

"Clean up that mess right now," said their mum.

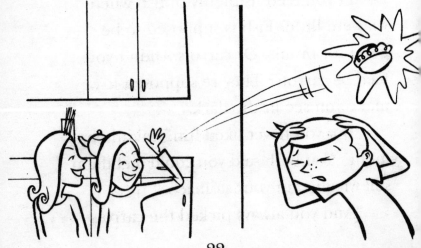

"But it's his fault," cried the twins. "He shouldn't have ducked!"

Oscar heard them still arguing as he hovered away to his bedroom to read the booklet Mr Robertson had given him about his new school.

The booklet had a picture of the School Of Greatly Gifted Youth on the outside. It showed a rather crumbly old house in the middle of an overgrown garden. A large cat sat on the steps leading up to the front door. The door was slightly open. Oscar immediately felt that he wanted to walk through that door. He felt that when he did the large cat would follow. The open door looked both welcoming and mysterious at the same time.

"I can hardly wait till tomorrow to go to S.O.G.G.Y. What a strange name for a school. I wonder who I'll meet there. I wonder what their special gifts will be.

I wonder what they'll think of me?" he said to himself, and decided to go to bed early, just like he did every Christmas Eve, so that the next day would come more quickly.

In bed he read the school timetable. It looked a bit strange. As well as all the usual stuff like Maths and Language there were classes on Puzzle-solving, Survival, Extra-acute Hearing, X-ray Vision, and Mind-reading.

"I wonder if I'll be any good at these things," wondered Oscar some more. "I wonder what kind of puzzles I'll have to solve. I wonder if we'll go out and live in wild places. I've only ever spent one night in a tent, and that was in the back garden. I wonder what extra-acute hearing is like. I wonder what x-ray vision is like . . ." And Oscar fell asleep still wondering.

Then he started to dream.

He dreamed of cats. Big cats, little cats, fat cats, skinny cats. Black cats, white cats, cats-go-out-in-the-night cats. He was in such a deep sleep that he didn't hear his mum come into his bedroom, pick up his duvet, and reach up to cover him with it. For, as often happened, Oscar was asleep three feet above his bed. This was very comfortable except when he came down to Earth with a bump, as he did at half-past seven next morning.

While he was cleaning his teeth he had another look at the booklet. It said the school rules were made up by the pupils. The rules were very sensible. Especially the one about school uniform. There wasn't any. Everyone could wear what they found most comfortable, whether it was camouflage trousers, tatty old jeans or the saggiest jumper in the world.

But no one was allowed to wear expensive trainers or designer ski jackets, just to show off.

"Suits me," grinned Oscar. "I haven't got anything flash to show off anyway."

So he went down to breakfast wearing his baggy old sweatshirt and washed-out jeans.

Evie and Angie were not pleased.

"We only get to dress like that on Casual Dress Day in our school, and then we have to pay twenty pence each for school funds. It's not fair!"

"Tough luck," grinned Oscar, and pinched the last slice of buttered toast when they weren't looking.

Then, still smiling, he put on his old trainers and said goodbye to his mum.

"You're sure you don't want me to come with you, Oscar?" she said, trying to smooth down his hair.

"No, I'll be fine, Mum. Honestly," said Oscar. "Mr Robertson has faxed the new school all my details, so they're expecting me." And he took his packed lunch from her, and set out, smiling, for S.O.G.G.Y.

CHAPTER FOUR

Oscar didn't really know what to expect at S.O.G.G.Y., so he wanted more time on his own to think. What would the teachers be like? Would they like him? He was excited and scared at the same time. Perhaps he should have let his mum come with him, but she would only fuss. His stomach kept doing little flips like he'd eaten jumping beans instead of toast for breakfast. But at least his feet stayed on the ground.

When he reached Beacham Road he could see the school at the far end. As he got closer it looked even crumblier than in the photo. Paint was peeling off the

the tall window frames, slates were missing from the roof, and chimney pots sat askew, giving the school a slightly comical look. But it looked really friendly, like it could surround Oscar in a big warm hug. As Oscar got closer still, a tall, slender woman came to the creaking gates to meet him.

S.O.C.C.Y.

"You must be Oscar," she smiled, holding out her hand. "I've been waiting for you. I had a feeling you would be early. I'm Madame Estella Carella."

Oscar liked her immediately. She had a gentle smile, a long rainbow-coloured dress, and messy piled-up hair with three pencils sticking out of it.

"I hope you'll like this school," Madame Estella said to him. "All the children here – well, nearly all – have special gifts. The teachers have, too, and are here to help you develop your talents as best you can. Then we hope, as you grow up, you'll use them to help other people. Now, do you like lemonade and cookies? I always think you should start a new school with lemonade and cookies, don't you?"

"Oh yes," said Oscar, and felt his spirits lift at the thought of this new

school. Then he felt the faint fizziness
in his feet and felt his body lift, too –
three feet into the air.

Madame Estella clapped her
hands in delight.

"Oh how splendid!" she said.

"You're our very first hoverer, Oscar.
You're going to be a real credit to the
school!"

Oscar grinned. A credit! Now that
sounded much better than a weirdo.
He followed Madame Estella up the
worn steps of the school, and there,
sitting on the top step, just as the
booklet had shown, was a large cat.

"This is Mystic Mog," explained
Madame Estella. "She's rather special,
too."

The large cat looked at Oscar,
and with a tinkling of the bell on her
blue collar, turned and followed him
through the school doorway.

Oscar followed Madame Estella through a series of long narrow passageways. A panel of old-fashioned bells hung above one of the doors at the end of an open passageway. Oscar had a closer look as he hovered past. The panel had names written on it in faded gold lettering. Names like Pantry and Drawing-room and Conservatory.

"This was once a very grand house," explained Madame Estella.

"My family used to to own it. They were very wealthy and had lots of servants. They used the bell-pushes in every room to call for morning coffee or afternoon tea. But the bells don't work now. Like so many other things in the school, I'm afraid."

Madame Estella opened the door to her study. Oscar and Mystic Mog followed her in. Like Madame Estella, the study was untidy and welcoming. Piles of books covered every surface. Some lay open with a pair of spectacles marking the place. Oscar counted at least six pairs, not including the three pairs Madame Estella wore on chains around her neck.

"Now, where did I put the lemonade and cookies?" she said. "I left them ready before I went out."

"I think they're on your desk." Oscar pointed, as Mystic Mog jumped up beside the cookies expectantly.

"Ah yes," said Madame Estella. "I can hardly see a thing without my glasses." And she felt about in her piled-up hair and brought down another pair that Oscar hadn't noticed. She put them on and poured out the lemonade. She gave Oscar a large glass and as he lifted the clear, sparkling liquid to his lips, he was almost sure he heard Mystic Mog say, "Cheers, Oscar!"

Oscar shook his head and bit into a delicious cookie. He had eaten three more, at Madame Estella's insistence, before she took him down some narrow passageways to his classroom. It was a large room with three tall windows and a high ceiling, flaking in places. Tiny particles of pale plaster floated in the morning sunshine. Old-fashioned wooden desks sat in rows facing the blackboard. Oscar sat down in one and it creaked loudly.

"This is where most of your discoveries will be," said Madame Estella.

"Discoveries?" said Oscar.

"That's what we call lessons here. A much nicer word than lessons, don't you think?"

Oscar nodded.

"I remember now. I saw that in the booklet," he said, as the classroom door opened and a dark-eyed girl and a round-faced boy came in.

"Ah, Gnatalie and Wibbly!" exclaimed Madame Estella. "Our two early birds. I want you to meet Oscar Smith. He's our first hoverer. I saw him hover earlier. Three feet up in the air. It was fantastic. But Oscar's bound to feel a bit strange in a new school, so I know you two will make him feel quite at home." And she gave them all a gentle smile and slipped away.

"Hi, Oscar," said the dark-eyed girl. "I'm Gnatalie, with a 'g' like gnat. My parents can't spell very well. Neither can I. But I do have x-ray vision, so that kind of makes up for it."

"Hullo, Oscar," said the round-faced boy. "I'm Walter Wobble, but everyone calls me Wibbly. I can read minds and I can tell you're really pleased to be here."

"Yes," grinned Oscar. "I think it's a great place. I just know I'm going to love everything."

"Well, perhaps not everything," said Gnatalie.

"Or everyone," said Wibbly.

But Oscar was too happy to notice. What he did notice was that when the faint feeling of fizziness started in his feet again and he rose slowly into the air, neither Gnatalie nor Wibbly batted an eyelid. No sliding to the ground in a dead faint. No rushing to phone the police. No shouts of "Alien Attack!" or "Weirdo Alert!" Just great big grins of welcome and exclamations of "Wow! Terrific!"

It was nice to feel normal at last.

CHAPTER FIVE

Soon the rest of the class piled in, laughing and talking. Gnatalie and Wibbly introduced Oscar.

"Hi," said one boy. "My name's Peter's Purbright, but everyone calls me Big-ears."

Oscar looked at his ears. They didn't look very big.

"I've got extra-acute hearing," explained Peter. "That's why they call me Big-ears. I know, if you can hover, why don't we call you Hover Boy?"

Oscar thought for a moment. "I like it," he grinned. "It's a bit like Superman. So long as no one expects me to wear my underpants on the outside."

Everyone laughed and slapped Oscar on the back. Hover Boy was born.

Oscar sat in the empty seat beside Gnatalie and Wibbly.

"When does the bell ring for lessons – I mean, discoveries?" he said.

"Oh, there aren't any bells," said Gnatalie. "Discoveries begin when everyone's here."

"Is everyone here?" asked Oscar, looking round.

"Not quite," said Wibbly, and made a face. "There's one more to come. Banger McGrath, the head boy."

Suddenly the classroom door banged open and a large untidy youth stood there. He wore a school uniform of grey trousers, blue blazer with white trim, and a whitish shirt and crumpled tie.

"Guess who had spaghetti bolognese for his dinner last night?" muttered Gnatalie to Oscar.

"Wow," said Oscar. "With your x-ray vision, can you see that in his stomach?"

"Don't have to," whispered Gnatalie. "I can see it on his tie."

Oscar looked at the blob of tomato sauce and curl of spaghetti on Banger's tie and grinned.

"What are *you* grinning at?" asked Banger, swooping down upon Oscar and poking him in the shoulder with a none-too-clean finger.

"Nothing," said Oscar.

"Oh, I see. Grinning at nothing.

40

Is that your special gift? Is that why you've come to this school? I can just see you on *Mastermind*. Specialist subject: Grinning at Nothing."

"Oscar can hover, Banger," said Wibbly quietly.

"Hoover?" said Banger. "Hoover? Is that his special gift? Housework!"

"Not *hoover*. Hover," said Gnatalie. "Hover, as in three feet above the ground."

"Nonsense," said Banger. "I've seen some weird goings-on in this school, but defying gravity? Complete nonsense. He's obviously a fake. How do you do it – with wires under your armpits or something?" And he poked at Oscar's sweatshirt to see if there was anything hidden there.

Oscar shook his head. "I don't know how I do it," he said. "It just happens."

"Like when?" sneered Banger. "When there's nobody looking, I bet."

41

Oscar felt the faint fizziness starting in his feet.

"No, like now," he said. He stood up and slowly rose three feet into the air.

"Wow!" said the rest of the class. "Brilliant. Magic. Awesome. Well done, Hover Boy, that showed him!"

Banger's mouth dropped open and he stood there in the middle of the classroom floor, staring.

The classroom door opened again more quietly and a small, chubby man with thick glasses butstled into the room. He looked at Oscar and Banger.

"Pick your chin up from the floor and sit down, Banger," he said. "Haven't you ever seen a hoverer before?"

"N-n-n-no, sir," said Banger.

"No, neither have I," said Mr Blister, whose nickname was Rumble, on account of his rumbling tum. "But when I was in India, perfecting my

Indian rope trick, I read about the possibility in an old book. I have it in my study somewhere. Anyway, welcome to S.O.G.G.Y., Oscar Smith. Please sit down. Whenever you can, that is."

The faint feeling of fizziness disappeared as quickly as it had come and Oscar bumped down to the floor and hit his knee on the old wooden desk.

"Hmm," said Mr Blister, making a note and stuffing it into a pocket in his multi-coloured waistcoat. "We must try to do something to help control these landings. Can't have Hover Boy with his legs in plaster."

The class giggled while Banger slunk to a seat behind Oscar.

Mr Blister took out the class register.

"Hands up anyone who's not here," he said.

The class smiled as they did every morning at his little joke and Mr Blister put the register away.

"Right," he said. "Today's discovery is Anatomy."

"This is very useful to me," said Gnatalie, "with my x-ray vision. When I'm looking through someone's body it helps if I can tell the difference between intestines and spaghetti!"

"Right," said Oscar, who wasn't really

sure he wanted to know about intestines. Then he gasped when Mr Blister opened a cupboard and wheeled out a skeleton.

"This is Fred, Oscar," he said. "Would you like to shake hands?"

Oscar gulped and held out a shaky hand. He was relieved to discover Fred's hand was plastic, although he could have sworn the skeleton grinned at him. "There is a rumour," went on Mr

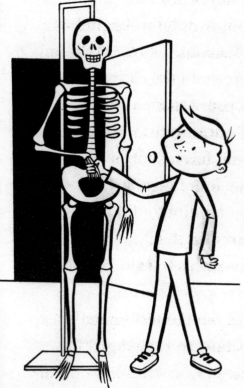

Blister, "that a long time ago Fred was a pupil at this school, but he forgot to do his homework and was locked in the cupboard as a punishment. Then he was forgotten about. *You* won't forget to do your homework, Oscar, will you?"

"No," grinned Oscar. "Certainly not!"

Mr Blister's eyes twinkled and he nodded. "Good. Now let us begin."

Oscar was fascinated by the Anatomy lesson. Mr Blister told the class to pair off and gave each pair a spatula.

"Now find out, carefully," he said, "if your partner still has his tonsils."

There was a lot of giggling and coughing and counting of fillings as the class got on with that.

Oscar still had his tonsils. Wibbly didn't.

Then it was time to test for reflexes and the spatulas were exchanged for tendon hammers.

"Tap the knees only," warned
Mr Blister.

Wibbly's reflexes were fine, as
Oscar discovered when Wibbly's foot
shot up and connected with Oscar's
nose.

"Oops, sorry," grinned Wibbly.

"'S'alride," grinned Oscar.

Then it was rib counting time.

"I didn't know I had twelve pairs,"
giggled Oscar, looking under his
sweatshirt at his skinny body. "And
I thought my heart was further round
to the side than it is. There is is there,
just above my left breastbone. Hullo,
little heart. *Hub dub, hub dub, hub dub.*
Now, whereabouts are my kidneys?
Here, kidney kidney, where are you?"

Time flew past as Oscar filled in the
little skeleton map Mr Blister had given
them with the names of different parts
of the body. It looked good, but not as

good as Wibbly's map. Wibbly had filled his in using his special pen. The pen wrote in three colours – red, blue and green – and his map was very colourful. Mr Blister collected the maps in, and his stomach gave a loud rumble.

"Good gracious. Is it that time already?" he said. "Time for a break, ladies and gentlemen. Go out into the garden and fill your lungs – you should know where they are by now – with some good fresh air. Then fill your stomachs with whatever dreadful food you have brought with you. I see you like Cheesy Crumbles, Hover Boy. Can that be the secret of your hovering? No doubt we shall find out . . . or maybe we won't." And he gave the class a small bow and left.

"So what did you think of your first discovery, Hover Boy?" asked Wibbly.

"Magic," said Oscar. "It's all so

different. Just show me where the kidneys would be on Fred again. I think I've got that wrong on my skeleton map. They're so clever, kidneys, aren't they, filtering out all the gunge in our bodies? But I don't think I could eat steak and kidney pie ever again. I hope my mum doesn't make any for tea."

CHAPTER SIX

At break-time, Gnatalie and Wibbly took Oscar to their favourite place in the overgrown school garden. It was round the back of the house, through a secret path beyond the bramble patch. There, in a little clearing, was an old oak which had been blown down in a winter gale. Most of its branches were gone and it made a great place to sit.

The friends got out their food, and shared Oscar's Cheesy Crumbles and Gnatalie's ketchup-flavoured crisps. They fed Wibbly's pumpernickel bread sandwiches to the crows who didn't

seem to mind the pickled walnut
and mince filling.

"Mum's always coming up with
strange sandwich fillings," sighed
Wibbly. "As well as exotic casseroles.
She makes them for a living."

"I like casseroles," said Oscar.
"We had a sausage one with mashed
potatoes last night. It was good."

"We had a lettuce, turnip and green pea one last night," said Wibbly. "It was awful."

"I had baked beans on toast," said Gnatalie, "which I made myself. Mum and Dad are always so busy with their sculptures, they sometimes forget I'm there. Never mind that I need to eat!"

"What are they making?" asked Oscar, who secretly wished his parents did interesting things like make exotic casseroles or sculptures, but his dad worked for a dairy and his mum had a part-time job in the local supermarket. But, at least, they never ran out of milk, though they did eat rather a lot of nearly past their sell-by date sausages.

"I don't know exactly what they're making," said Gnatalie, screwing up her face. "It's difficult to tell. The front end looks like a Jersey cow and the back end like a double-decker bus.

In between it's a bit like the big dipper
at the fair."

"Oh," said Oscar. "That sounds
. . . interesting."

"It's not so interesting when you
discover your favourite chair's been
chopped up for the sculpture. I lock
my bedroom door now, just in case they
chop up my bed while I'm out." And
she showed them a heavy iron key on a
chain round her neck. "Though," she
added gloomily, "they'll probably chop
up the bedroom door, too. The door to
the loo's already gone."

Oscar looked appalled. "So what
do you do then if you go . . . I mean,
if you need . . . I mean if you want a . . .
bath?"

"Sing very loudly," said Gnatalie.
"A good long soak takes up all the pop
songs I know."

They were just discussing their

favourite pop groups when there
was a crash and a yell.

"That's Banger," grinned Wibbly.
"He's always trying to find out where
Gnatalie and I disappear to at break
and lunchtime, but he doesn't know the
secret path. He's probably ripped his
trousers on the brambles again. Come
on, we'll nip back to the front of the
school and pretend we've been there
all the time."

"Why is Banger so nasty?" asked
Oscar on the way back.

"Because he's here on false
pretences," said Gnatalie. "He doesn't
have any special gifts."

"His dad owns the school," said
Wibbly. "He bought it from Madame
Estella when she couldn't afford to
run it anymore. He was going to knock
it down and build a block of flats, so
Madame Estella had to tell him about

the pupils having special gifts.

"Then he changed his mind and sent Banger here to keep an eye on us, and to see if he could somehow learn special gifts, too. His dad hopes that might make him even more money. Madame Estella has to let Banger be head boy to keep his dad happy and to keep the school open."

"These awful clothes Banger wears belong to his dad," said Gnatalie. "He makes him wear the old school uniform he had as a boy."

"Oh no," said Oscar, and began to feel rather sorry for Banger, even if he was horrible.

The discovery after break was Mind-reading. It was taken by Professore Allegore.

"Well, Banger," said the Professore. "I have travelled the world with my mind-reading act. I have astounded people from Adelaide to Zanzibar, but I don't need any of my amazing skills to see that you've been in the bramble patch again."

Banger scowled. His hands were scratched, his trousers were torn and there was a purple juice stain on his nose.

"Don't sit down," the Professore said. "See if you can tell me what's written on this card." And he produced a white card from his sleeve, as if by magic.

Banger looked hard at the white card the Professore held up.

"I can't see anything," he muttered.

"The mind has many secrets to reveal to us, Banger. Don't look with your eyes. Look with your mind," said the Professore kindly. "On the side of the card I am looking at there is a simple picture. I am concentrating on this picture, Banger. It is in my mind. Look there and tell me what you see."

Banger screwed up his eyes and looked at the Professore. He saw a tall man with a tanned face and a shock of ripply white hair that seemed to grow up to a point at the top of his head.

"I see," said Banger. "I see . . . an ice-cream cone."

"Interesting," said the Professore, "but incorrect."

He turned the white card round and showed the class the picture. It was of a large, old-fashioned bath.

"Better luck next time," said the Professore. "Now let's try you, Oscar Smith – or Hover Boy, as I believe you are sometimes called."

The Professore produced a white card from his other sleeve. Oscar tried to look with his mind and not with his eyes. It wasn't easy. His mind was a blank. Then he thought about the old bath.

"A rubber duck," he suggested hopefully.

The Professore laughed. "A good guess," he said. "But wrong." And he turned the card round to show a wigwam.

"Now, Wibbly," he said. "Since you are our expert, a hard one for you." And he held up another white card which seemed to come from nowhere.

Wibbly frowned, then grinned.

"The card is blank," he said. "There's nothing on it."

"Ah, Wibbly," said the Professore, turning round the blank card. "It seems I cannot trick you at all."

The Professore then told the class to split up into pairs. "This is what I did in my act," he beamed. "I will give each pair some playing cards. Then you will face your partner and hold up one playing card at a time. Concentrate hard on it and your partner will try to read the card in your mind."

"You'll be my partner, Hover Boy," said Banger, and sat down in front of Oscar before he could protest.

They held up the cards for each other and noted down the score.

Banger took great delight in shouting out, "Wrong, Hover Boy!" to each of Oscar's guesses.

When the Professore asked about the

scores, Banger said triumphantly, "I got three right. Hover Boy got none!"

The Professore passed on to Wibbly who had a perfect score.

"Well done, Wibbly," said Oscar, and was just patting him on the back when the faint feeling of fizziness started in his feet and he rose three feet into the air and hovered there.

"*Molto bene*," cried the Professore, gazing up at Oscar. "Very good!"

Oscar smiled and gave a little bow.

"Show off," muttered Banger McGrath. "I'll soon show you what happens to show offs." And he stood up quickly and dropped his playing cards. He gathered them up quickly, but not before Oscar saw that Banger had lied. Oscar *had* guessed some correctly.

Oscar shrugged and said nothing. It had been a great first day at S.O.G.G.Y. There was so much to do, so much to learn, so much to enjoy. He was determined not to let Banger McGrath spoil it.

CHAPTER SEVEN

Oscar's mum was at the front door waiting for him when he got home.

"There you are," she said, giving him a quick hug. "I've been thinking about you all day, wondering how you were getting on at your new school."

"I got on fine," said Oscar. "I'll tell you all about it over tea. What are we having? I'm starving."

Over his fish and chips Oscar told his family all about Gnatalie and Wibbly and Banger McGrath, and about the teachers, Fred, the skeleton, and the discoveries.

"Discoveries! Why can't you have

ordinary lessons like the rest of us.
Right bunch of weirdos you're mixed
up with now," said Evie and Angie.
"You should have stayed at our school.
We're putting on a Christmas panto.
We've got leading parts. We're going
to be famous."

"What's the panto?" asked Oscar.

"*Cinderella.*"

"Bet you're the ugly sisters," grinned
their brother.

"How did you know that?" they said.

"Easy. Just look in the mirror."

Evie and Angie kicked him under
the table.

"Stop that, you lot," said their mum.
"Or there'll be no chocolate cake for
afters. And speaking of cakes," she went
on, "it'll be your birthday soon, Oscar.
Have you decided what you'd like to do
for it?"

Oscar shook his head. "Dunno."

"Well, I'm not going on the steam railway with him again," said Evie. "I got my face covered in sooty specks the last time."

"And I'm not going paddling with him again in October," said Angie. "My toes turned blue. So don't come up with any more crazy ideas. I don't see why he can't just have a party like the rest of us."

"A party," said Oscar, hovering quickly into the air and upsetting the table and the tea things. "Oh I don't think I'd like a party."

"Why not?" said his mum. "Now that you're at this new school I phoned the family and told them about your special gift. You don't need to keep it a secret anymore. Not from them, anyway."

"We could have the family round," said his dad, picking up the fallen crockery. "And, providing we've got

enough tea cups left, you could
invite some friends as well."

"Mmm, I don't know," said Oscar,
hovering just above the television.
"I suppose I could invite Gnatalie
and Wibbly."

"I could make a cake and do
sausage rolls and those little sausages
on sticks that you like," said his mum.

"Boring," said Evie. "Why doesn't he have a super intergalactic birthday party and I could come as the lovely princess Glitterata from the planet Stardust."

"And I could come as the even lovelier princess Pansypops from the planet Flowerdew."

Oscar stopped hovering abruptly and fell sideways on to the sofa.

"Perhaps it would be nice to have a birthday party, Mum," he said, "now that I've made new friends. But an ordinary one will be fine."

"Some people," sniffed Evie and Angie, "have no imagination. It'll be a terrible bore, but perhaps we won't have to be there. Perhaps we'll be abducted by handsome aliens overcome by our beauty before then."

"We can always hope," said Oscar.

* * *

Oscar mentioned the party to Gnatalie and Wibbly in school next day.

"I'd love to come!" said Gnatalie.

"Me, too," said Wibbly.

"The only thing is," said Oscar, hovering up and down the school gardens and bumping into low-slung branches, "my relatives don't do anything very exciting. They just eat, sleep, and watch the telly mostly."

"Sounds good to me," said Gnatalie.

"And me," said Wibbly. "Do you know I had a mung bean casserole instead of a cake last year because Mum completely forgot about my birthday till the last minute? Have you ever tried sticking candles in a mung bean casserole?"

Oscar laughed and bumped gently down to earth. He needn't have worried. This was going to be a great birthday party.

CHAPTER EIGHT

Next day, on the way to school, Oscar's wellies sprung a leak.

"Oh no," said Oscar. "Now, if I could hover whenever I wanted to, I could avoid all these puddles."

When he got to school he went in search of the cloakroom to take off his wellies. He finally found it after a long trek through the winding passageways from the front door of the school to the back. Like most other things at S.O.G.G.Y. the cloakroom was rather unusual. It was long and narrow with dark wood panelling. Rows of coat pegs ran along the two long walls.

Above the coat pegs hung big game trophies. Lion and tiger heads, and rhino and buffalo heads stared fiercely at Oscar as he tried to take off his wellies.

"I wish someone would invent an easy way to remove leaky wellies," he muttered, as he struggled with them.

At that moment the faint feeling of fizziness started in his damp feet, and he shot up three feet into the air.

"Oh no," he cried. "It's even more difficult to get my wellies off up here."

Then, just as quickly as it had come, the faint feeling of fizziness went away. But Oscar stayed where he was. He didn't drift gently to the ground as he sometimes did. Instead he just stayed where he was, swinging gently, with the back of his anorak caught on the end of the rhino's horn.

"Help," he yelled. "Get me down.

I'm being attacked by a rhino. Help!"

The cloakroom door banged open and in came, Banger McGrath.

"Well, well, well," he said. "Not quite so clever now, Hover Boy, caught hanging around in the cloakroom. Your special gift's got you into trouble."

"Never mind that, Banger," said Oscar. "Help me to get down."

"Don't know if I want to," said

Banger. "Think I'll just close the door and leave you here to starve. You're pretty skinny as it is. Shouldn't take you long to turn into a skeleton. Just like Fred. Ha ha ha!"

"Don't be stupid, Banger. Help me down."

"How much is it worth?"

"I don't have any money."

"We'll soon see about that," said Banger, and was just going through Oscar's pockets when the door opened and Madame Estella came in.

"Something told me there was something wrong here," she frowned. "Then I thought I heard yells."

"You did," said Banger quickly. "I heard them too and came running. Oscar's got caught up in the rhino's horn. I was just helping him down."

"I see," Madame Estella looked thoughtful. "Poor Oscar. How awful to

71

get stuck up there. Banger, go and ask Mr Periwinke, the caretaker, to come and take these horrible trophies down immediately." Banger gave Oscar a look that said "Tell tales and I'll thump you" and went off.

"I know these trophies are dreadful things," said Madame Estella, examining Oscar's ripped anorak, "but not as dreadful as my ancestors who shot the poor animals in the first place. I suppose I should throw them out, but, do you know, I haven't the heart to put the poor creatures out in the rain. But I am so glad you're all right, Oscar."

Oscar nodded. No thanks to Banger, he thought.

"There is so much to learn about your hovering," went on Madame Estella, "Everyone in the school benefits by knowing more about all the special gifts. I wonder, now that you've settled

in so well and so quickly, if you'd
mind being the star of a discovery
today, and letting your class find
out as much as they can about your
special gift?"

Me, a star, thought Oscar. Wow!

Out loud he said, "I wouldn't mind
at all, Madame Estella. I'd like to know
more about it myself."

"Good," beamed Madame Estella.
"Now let's get you out of these wet
wellies then you can go along to the
classroom and tell Mr Blister that
you'll be happy to be the subject of
the discovery."

Mr Blister was delighted.

"Good boy, Oscar," he said. "Please
go and stand in front of the class and
let them observe you."

Oscar stood and faced the class.
He felt strange with everyone looking

at him. It didn't help that Wibbly pulled silly faces and Gnatalie wiggled her ears. Oscar tried to swallow his laughter, but it only made his face hot, his throat dry and his ears pop. But worse was to come.

"First of all, describe what this boy looks like," Mr Blister said to the class.

"Skinny," sneered Banger.

"Freckly," said Big Ears.

"Knobbly-kneed," laughed everyone.

"Now you may ask him questions," said Mr Blister.

At first the questions were quite sensible.

"How old were you the first time you hovered?"

"Can you hover when you want?"

"Can the rest of your family hover, too?"

Then the questions got a bit silly.

"Do you have big feet?"

"Are they both the same size?"

"Are they smelly?"

Mr Blister stopped the questions there and asked Oscar to lie on the table and let the class have a look at his feet.

Oscar took off his damp socks and climbed on to the table. The class gathered round.

"Well that answers one question,"

said Wibbly. "His feet are definitely smelly."

The class measured Oscar's feet. They counted the number of toes and checked in between them for bits of fluff. Verdict: very ordinary feet. Then they took it in turns to tickle his feet to see how long he could last without giggling. Verdict: three seconds.

By this time Oscar couldn't stop giggling and the whole class joined in. All except Banger McGrath. All the attention Oscar was getting really annoyed him and he make a grab for Oscar's right foot.

"Let me have a proper look at his stupid feet," he said.

At that moment though, the faint fizziness started and he hovered up horizontally and clunked his foot on Banger's chin.

"Oops, sorry, Banger," grinned Oscar.

The class exploded, and there was so much laughing that Mr Blister nearly didn't hear his stomach rumble. When he did they all tumbled outside, still giggling.

"That was brilliant fun," the class said to Oscar. "Well done, Hover Boy."

Banger scowled at Oscar. "It's not fair," he muttered. "I should be getting that attention. I'm the head boy around here. My dad owns the school." Banger scowled even more and thrust his hands deep into his blazer pockets. "That Oscar Smith needs taking down a peg or two. Pity he's not still hanging up in the cloakroom."

Oscar saw Banger scowl at him and felt uneasy. Banger had obviously taken an instant dislike to him, and the clunk on his chin hadn't helped either. Oscar now had no doubt that Banger would be out to get him.

CHAPTER NINE

Oscar was right.

All the way home that day Banger wondered how he could get back at Oscar. While he was thinking about it he kicked tin cans along the street, chased cats up trees and barked at dogs – small dogs. Poodles and Yorkshire terriers, mostly. He gave big dogs a wide berth. He went into the supermarket and bought a load of ice cream, sweets and crisps. Stuffing his face usually helped him think. He was halfway down his second ice cream when he thought of a plan.

"Of course," he yelled out loud.

"It's so simple."

An old lady, who was passing, thought he was yelling at her, and bopped him with her umbrella.

Banger hardly noticed. He was too busy thinking about his plan.

It was brilliant. Utterly brilliant. He was brilliant to have thought of it. He ate two packets of crisps to celebrate his brilliance and thought about it some more. It involved Wibbly's special pen.

His mum had given it to him one birthday, before she started being an exotic cookery book writer, before she started being famous, before she started forgetting his birthday. Wibbly used it all the time. It made his note books very colourful. Banger really liked that pen, but Wibbly got very cross and upset if anyone borrowed it.

"And that's just what I'll do," grinned Banger. "I'll *borrow* it and slip it into Hover Boy's pocket. Then I'll accuse him of stealing it. That'll soon put an end to everyone thinking he is so wonderful. Might even get him expelled if I speak to my dad!"

And Banger went home so pleased with his plan that he passed a tin can, two cats and three dogs without noticing them.

CHAPTER TEN

In the meantime, Oscar's mum had
been busy.

"I bought birthday party invitations
for you today," she told Oscar at the tea
table. "They were 'reduced for quick
sale' in the shop."

Oscar looked at the invitations.
He could see why. The bluebirds and
robins on them were chirping, "It'll
be a real *tweet* if you come to my
Birthday Party." They would do Hover
Boy's street cred no good at all!

"Wasn't there anything else a
bit more grown up, Mum?" he asked.
"Perhaps with aliens or spaceships

or something?"

"Don't you like them?" asked his mum.

"They're gross," snorted Angie and Evie. "We wouldn't be seen dead giving out invitations like that."

Oscar looked at his mum's hurt expression.

"The invitations are fine," he lied.

"Good," said his mum. "You can write them out tonight and take them into school for your friends tomorrow. I'll post the others off to Uncle George and Auntie Vera."

Oscar looked again at the invitations. Perhaps if he cut the tails off the bluebirds and the heads off the robins they wouldn't look so bad. But, in the end, he left them as they were, since it was nice of his mum to buy them.

Gnatalie and Wibbly were delighted to get their invitations.

"Cool, Hover Boy," said Gnatalie.
"I'm looking forward to meeting
your parents and these weird sisters
of yours."

"Nice invitation. I love the robins.
I love birthday parties too," said Wibbly.
"I remember when I used to have them
. . . well I remember having one." And
he took out his special three-coloured
pen and put it on his desk.

"There'll be plenty to eat at the
party," said Oscar. "Mum's doing
sausages on sticks and birthday cake,
on separate plates, just to be posh!"

The three friends laughed and while
they were deep in conversation about
what they might buy Oscar for his
birthday, Banger sneaked up. He saw
his chance to carry out his plan. He
pocketed Wibbly's special pen. He
grinned, well pleased with himself.
It only took a moment later on to

accidentally bump into Oscar and drop the pen into his pocket.

Then Banger sat back and waited for the fun to begin. He waited and waited, but nothing happened. When the next discovery began, Wibbly borrowed a pen from Gnatalie and calmly did his work.

Banger couldn't understand it. This was all wrong. This wasn't supposed to happen. Why wasn't Wibbly upset? Why wasn't he turning the classroom upside down to look for his precious pen? Why wasn't he demanding everyone's pockets be searched?

Banger stood it for as long as he could, then, just before lunchtime, he could stand it no longer. He sidled up to Wibbly.

"Lost anything recently, Wibbly?" he asked.

Wibbly blinked at him through his big glasses and searched his pockets. "No, I don't think so," he said. "Why, have you found something of mine, Banger?"

"I haven't," cried Banger in triumph. "But I think sticky fingers Hover Boy has. Earlier on I saw him put your three-coloured pen into his pocket."

"No, you didn't," said Wibbly quietly. "You took the pen, Banger. You put it into Oscar's pocket to cause trouble."

"I didn't. I wouldn't. You can't prove that," blustered Banger. "You didn't see me."

"I didn't have to," said Wibbly. "I read your mind. I told Oscar what you were going to do, and sure enough you did it."

"Aaaaargh!" Banger made a noise like an exploding duck and stomped off.

Oscar, who'd been keeping an eye on what was happening, grinned and handed Wibbly back his pen.

"Wow, that was great, Wibbly. How do you do that mind-reading thing?"

"I don't know," said Wibbly. "How do you do that hovering thing?"

"I don't know either," grinned Oscar.

"Perhaps one of these days we'll find out," they both said.

CHAPTER ELEVEN

The day of the birthday arrived. Oscar's mum had made a huge birthday cake. Actually she had made three, but the first one collapsed in the middle and the second one was burnt round the edges. They had both been fed to the birds. There were now some very fat sparrows in Oscar's garden. But birthday cake – mark three looked good. Oscar's mum had piped "Happy Birthday, Oscar" on the top in blue icing. Evie and Angie had stuck on some candles, mainly to hide the bits of icing they had pinched.

Oscar's dad had strung a banner

up across the sitting-room saying "Happy Birthday, Hover Boy" and had given him a nice fat envelope with some money in it.

"That's for the new Playstation I know you'd like," he said. "I thought we might go together to choose it."

"Thanks, Dad," said Oscar, who knew his dad must have had to save up hard for the present.

Oscar's mum gave him new jeans so his ankles wouldn't show at his new school. Evie and Angie gave him a gift token and told him to be sure to buy their favourite CD with it.

In the middle of the afternoon the guests started to arrive. Uncle George puffed in and bagged the best chair by the fire. He lowered himself into it carefully with the words, "Did I ever tell you about the time . . ."

"Yes," said everyone.

"Well, I'll tell you again anyway. A good story's worth repeating."

Auntie Vera came next, dressed in several hand-knitted jumpers and scarves, and complaining about how cold it was outside. After she'd taken off some of the jumpers and scarves she'd shrunk to about half her width. She pressed a soft squidgy parcel into Oscar's hands.

"Open it later, dear," she said. "I bet you can't guess what's inside."

"Bet you can," whispered Evie and Angie.

"Bet it's another of her horrible knitted jumpers. Perhaps it'll have 'H.B.' on the front for Hover Boy, but you'll need to have arms as long as Ape Man to fit it!"

But Oscar said "Thank you" politely and went to open the door to Gnatalie and Wibbly. He hardly recognized them, they were both so clean and bright and shiny.

"My mum's latest exotic casserole exploded," explained Wibbly. "So we had to clean up the kitchen. Then we had to clean up me."

"My mum and dad were thinking about using the bath in their new sculpture," said Gnatalie, "so I had to stay in there until they got a better idea. I'm as wrinkly as a prune under my clothes."

"You both look great," grinned Oscar. "Come and meet the others."

Gnatalie and Wibbly met Evie and Angie first. The twins peered at them from under all their eye make-up.

"You *look* all right," said Evie. "Quite normal really."

"If a bit boring," said Angie. "Have you never thought of having pink hair or green eye shadow or having a transfer of a tiger on your bum?"

"Not really," said Gnatalie.

"Not at all," said Wibbly.

Then Oscar's mum appeared and took them to meet the grown ups.

"Ah," said Uncle George to Gnatalie. "I've heard all about you. You're the girl with x-ray vision at Oscar's new school. Well, I've always liked a good story and there's one right under my nose. Imagine Oscar being able to hover and you being able to see through things. But I bet you can't tell me what's inside this box

I've got for Oscar's birthday."

Gnatalie looked. "Football boots," she said.

"Well, I never," said Uncle George. "You *can* see through things after all."

Gnatalie grinned. "I can also read labels. It says football boots on the box."

Auntie Vera laughed. "I told him they were a silly present for a boy who spends half his time with his feet in the air. I don't know where Oscar gets hovering from, either. There was never anything funny on our side of the family. Maybe it's to do with the hole in the ozone layer. I do hope Oscar doesn't disappear up through it. But I do like your jumper, dear. Did your mum knit it for you?"

"No," said Gnatalie. "I traded one of mum's old sculptures for it in Oxfam."

"*Oxfam*," squeaked Evie and Angie. "We wouldn't be seen dead in a charity shop!"

"They've got some good things in there," said Gnatalie. "That's where I got Oscar's present."

And she handed over a small box neatly wrapped in shiny blue paper. Inside was a new-looking leather belt and on the heavy metal buckle the initials "H.B." were inscribed.

"I bought the belt and got my dad to do the initials for you," said Gnatalie. "I hope you like it."

"Like it? I love it," said Oscar. "It'll hold up the new jeans Mum got me for school."

Then Wibbly handed over his parcel. It was a little one, too; long and narrow.

"It's a pen like mine," said Wibbly before Oscar could open it. "I thought you'd like one, too."

"Great idea, Wibbly," said Oscar. "Thank you."

He piled his presents up on a kitchen chair and went to help his mum. She was carrying a large plateful of sausages. The sausages seemed to have a life of their own and kept making big bids for freedom off the edge of the plate.

"Time for tea, everyone," called Oscar's mum. "What do you want to start with?"

"You can have anything you like," whispered Oscar. "So long as it's sausages."

"We love sausages," said Gnatalie and Wibbly.

When they were all full of hot dogs, sausage rolls and sausage on sticks, Oscar's dad decided it was time to play some party games.

"*Boring*," said Evie and Angie. "That's kids' stuff. We're not playing."

"Up to you," said their dad. "But I think we'll have a competition for the best disco dancer with a two-pound coin to the winner."

"We'll play, we'll play," cried the twins. "We're easily the best."

But they had some competition.

Auntie Vera took off another jumper and did a forward somersault and then the splits. Oscar's mum and dad did some rock and roll while

Gnatalie and Wibbly jumped around
till they were dizzy. Uncle George
was the judge and he kept time to
the music with his stick. Oscar, in
the meantime, felt the faint fizziness
start in his feet and danced in the
air three feet above the ground. He
was fine till his head hit the light
shade and sent it swinging wildly.

"It's just like disco lights," cried
Gnatalie. "Well done, Hover Boy."

Everyone laughed and after they
had all fallen to the floor, tired out,
Uncle George awarded the two-pound
coin to Wibbly because he had the
reddest face.

"Good lad, Wibbly," said Oscar's
mum. "Now we'll have some birthday
cake."

"We'll cut it, we'll cut it," cried the
twins, and rushed to the table.

When they handed Wibbly his piece,
they said. "Can you really read minds?"

"Uh huh," said Wibbly.

"Bet you don't know what we are
thinking now."

Wibbly looked at them and at his
piece of cake. "You're thinking if you
just cut small pieces of birthday cake for
everyone else there'll be more left for
you later."

"No, we're not," cried the twins and blushed till their faces were as pink as their hair.

"Very nice cake," said Wibbly, taking a mouthful. He grinned when they gave him another bit.

Oscar was really pleased at how well the party had gone. Gnatalie was talking to his mum and telling her about her parents' sculptures. Uncle George and Dad were talking to Wibbly and telling him about their coin collections. Evie and Angie were talking to themselves as usual, and fighting over the last sausage roll. Oscar hovered round, batting balloons at everyone and feeling happy.

Then he heard a clatter from the kitchen and the back door bang.

"What was that?" said his mum and dad.

"Probably the wind," said Oscar.
"I'll go and see."

He hovered out into the hall and
down into the kitchen. It was untidy
with the remains of the party food and
the back door was swinging open.
Oscar was just closing it when an
upturned chair caught his eye. It was
the chair where he'd left his birthday
presents. But the presents were gone.

CHAPTER TWELVE

"Oh no," said Oscar. "The wind didn't do this. We've been burgled!"

The others heard Oscar yell and rushed into the kitchen. "Someone's broken in and stolen my presents," he said. "But he can't be far away yet."

He hovered quickly in the garden and looked down the street. A man in a black bomber jacket was hurrying away.

"I wonder . . ." said Oscar. "But you can't run up to someone and demand to search their pockets."

"Wait," said Wibbly and fixed his eyes on the man. "He's thinking about heading for the train station."

"Come on," said Oscar. "We'll follow him."

Oscar fell to the ground and the three friends set off in pursuit.

"I wonder if he really is the thief," panted Oscar.

"He is," said Gnatalie, as they got closer. "I can see your presents, and a lot more, stuffed down his jacket.

"Right," said Oscar. "Take the short cut round the back of the baker's and head him off."

They ran pell mell through the precinct, dodging prams and skateboards, and hurtled down the narrow passageway behind The Crunchy Crust baker's. They almost knocked over Banger McGrath who was coming out of the baker's stuffing a large chocolate éclair into his mouth.

"We're chasing a robber, Banger,"

panted Oscar. "Come and help us catch him."

"No fear," said Banger. "Chase him yourself." And he hurried off the other way.

The man in the black bomber jacket was just coming into view. Gnatalie took out her mobile phone and phoned the police.

"Mum and Dad always make me carry it for emergencies," she puffed. "I usually use it to dial for a pizza."

The three friends hid in the passageway until the man was upon them. Then they leapt out.

"What . . . waaaa—" he yelled as he toppled over.

Wibbly sat heavily on his chest while Gnatalie tied his shoe laces together. Oscar felt the faint fizziness start in his feet and rose above him. He hovered there, dancing and yelling, just like he'd done at the party.

A crowd gathered round to watch.

"How does he do that?" they wondered. "It's a great trick. He should be on the telly."

"Help! Help! This man's a robber," yelled Oscar. "He stole my birthday presents. They're in his jacket!"

"Maybe he *is* on the telly," said the

crowd. "I wonder what they are filming. Must be one of these magic shows. Can you see where the camera is?"

The fizziness in Oscar's feet disappeared and he thumped down on to the man, just as a policeman made his way quickly through the crowd. He searched the man's bulging jacket. There were gold chains and CDs as well as Oscar's presents.

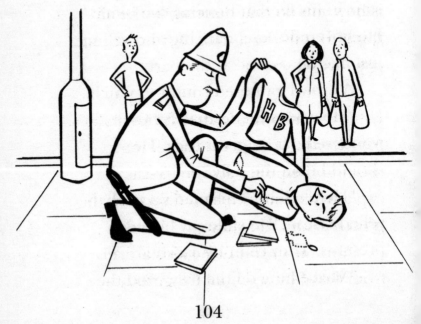

There was no mistaking Oscar's presents, especially Auntie Vera's sweater with "H.B." knitted on the front.

The policeman smiled at the man.

"We've been looking for you for some time, Sunshine. You're nicked. And you three," he said to the friends. "Down to the station with your parents. You've got some explaining to do, and the first thing I want to know is how you do that dancing in the air thing. It must be a trick, but I don't see any wires."

Later that evening Oscar and Gnatalie's parents and Wibbly's mum all went down to the police station. Oscar explained about the birthday party, the presents, and the chase.

"You mean you three kids are all from that funny school for gifted

105

children," said the policeman. "And you caught the robber using your special gifts?"

"Yes," said Oscar. "But it's a school rule that we don't boast about it or tell everyone."

"But you can really hover in the air?"

"Yes," said Oscar.

"And you really have got x-ray vision?" he asked Gnatalie.

"Yes," said Gnatalie.

"And you really can read minds?" he asked Wibbly.

"Yes," said Wibbly.

"Right," said the policeman suspiciously. "What am I thinking right now?"

"You're thinking you're far too old for all this nonsense, and you'd like to go home, put your feet up and have a nice cup of tea," grinned Wibbly.

"Let's all go home to our house and have a nice cup of tea," said Oscar's mum. "Who knows, there might even be some birthday cake left, if the twins haven't scoffed the lot."

Evie and Angie were furious at having missed all the excitement, and Auntie Vera wanted to hear the story of the robbery over and over again. Even Uncle George said the story was as good as any of his.

"Well, Oscar," said his mum and dad when they were all sitting round the fire drinking tea. "That was quite a birthday party."

Oscar grinned. Wibbly's mum looked thoughtful.

"Perhaps you'd like a birthday party too, Walter," she said. "I could make some special birthday casseroles."

"And a cake," said Wibbly. "You can't put candles in a casserole."

"Perhaps you could have a birthday party too, Gnatalie," said her mum and dad. "Everyone could bring their own junk and make a sculpture."

"And I could phone for pizzas," grinned Gnatalie.

Oscar looked round and gave a happy sigh. What a birthday! But it didn't end there.

At assembly the following Monday morning, Madame Estella told the school how she had been informed by the police that Oscar's hovering, aided by Gnatalie's x-ray vision and Wibbly's mind-reading, had helped to catch a thief.

"That's how I hope you will all use your special gifts," she said. "Not to show off, but to help others and to right wrongs whenever possible."

Banger scowled. He was furious with himself. Why hadn't he gone to help Oscar when he'd been asked?

The school gave three cheers for the three friends, but Banger glared at Oscar. Oscar felt Banger's eyes boring into him and caught the glare,

but he didn't care. He was happy
with his new school. He was happy with
his new friends. He was really happy to
be Hover Boy. He would worry about
Banger McGrath some other time.

MORE ADVENTURES FOR . . .

BEAT THE BULLY

If Banger doesn't learn a special gift of
his own, his dad might close the school down.
Can Hover Boy, Gnatalie and Wibbly
think of a plan before it's too late?

MISSING MOGGY MYSTERY

Hover Boy's secret is out, but there's
a new problem – Mystic Mog is missing.
Who would catnap Mystic Mog? Oscar
and his friends are determined to
find out!

ABOUT THE AUTHOR

MARGARET RYAN

was born and brought up in Paisley, Scotland, in a house full of books. She enjoyed writing, too, but didn't become a full-time writer until she had married and had brought up her two children, and been a teacher. Then, one day, she saw an advertisement in her local paper for a writers' group and joined up. Her writing career began!

Since then, Margaret has published many bestselling books for children of all ages, and in 2000, she won a Scottish Arts Council Book Award. Today she loves meeting her readers and is greatly in demand for her lively storytelling sessions. She lives with her husband in an old mill just outside St Andrews. The area is rich in wildlife, which Margaret hopes will be a great source of ideas . . .